X-MEN

HAVOK: The Secret of Cyclops' Brother

adapted by Francine Hughes
based on comic books by Roy Thomas and Arnold Drake
illustrated by Aristides Ruiz and
Dana and Del Thompson

Random House New York

L adies and gentlemen," said the president of Landon College to an audience of relatives and friends, "I present to you the graduating class."

Among the graduates was Alex Summers. Little did young Alex know, as he stepped up to the podium, that today he would be receiving more than just a diploma.

Alex scanned the audience. Somewhere out there was his older brother Scott and a group of Scott's friends. What Alex didn't know was that those friends were X-Men and that Scott was Cyclops, their leader.

Out in the audience, Scott turned to his companions. "Alex made a name for himself as a campus athlete," he told his girlfriend, Jean Grey, and Hank McCoy, the Beast. "No doubt he has *some* mutant blood in him. But I'm proudest about his graduating third in his class."

After the ceremony, Scott introduced Alex to his friends. He made no mention of their being X-Men. "Now get out of that cap and gown, little brother, and let's celebrate."

Alex headed back to his dorm room to change. He had just walked through the door when two men dressed in the garb of ancient Egyptians sprang out of nowhere! One grabbed him from behind, while the other sprayed him with a fine mist—*phssst!*—from a scarab ring.

"What the...?" But before Alex could finish, his eyes closed and he fell to the ground.

When Alex didn't return, the X-Men went to the dorm to find him. They found only his cap, lying on the ground.

Jean focused her psionic powers on finding Alex.

At the same moment, not too far away, Alex regained consciousness. He was shackled to a marble slab in some sort of Egyptian chamber! Mummy cases lined the hieroglyphics-marked walls, and a man in a robe and golden helmet stood over him.

"Here lies the only man who can challenge my power," bellowed the man. He lifted a jeweled knife above Alex's chest. "And I, the last Living Pharaoh, ordain his death!"

Suddenly a beam of light, like a scarlet lightning bolt, flashed at the knife. It was Cyclops, shooting his optic blast!

The knife shattered like glass. "Now you must all perish!" the Pharaoh shouted, turning to face Cyclops and the rest of the X-Men. "Behold my magic." He tossed a charm in their direction that filled the room with smoke.

"Magic, my foot!" said Beast, diving for the Pharaoh but missing in the haze. "He's a mutant, same as us!"

The Pharaoh, meanwhile, had pressed a button, releasing the mummy cases and filling the room with Egyptian warriors.

"And so it comes to this, man of flaming eyes," the Pharaoh said to Cyclops. "Your mutant power against my own."

The Pharaoh let loose a powerful blast from his fingertips. Cyclops shot off a blast of his own. But his optic beam bounced right back at him!

"My wall of sound," laughed the Pharaoh. "Your powers cannot penetrate it!"

Then, using the wall of sound for protection, the Pharaoh and his warriors escaped.

"We'll deal with them later," Cyclops told the X-Men. "First, let me get these shackles off my brother."

"Brother?" said Alex. He shook his head. "Did you say *brother*? Scott, is that you?"

Beast led the X-Men away so Cyclops and Alex could be alone.

"It's funny," Cyclops began. "I've been waiting all these years to level with you, and now... I don't know what to say."

Alex grinned. "What's the matter? You afraid I'm going to be ashamed of being the kid brother of the leader of the X-Men? Cyclops or Scott—you're still the greatest!"

And then suddenly the Pharaoh was back!

"I bring with me the curse of the Pharaoh's eyes!" he shrieked.

Cyclops looked up. The Pharaoh's eyes had turned into hypnotic gems. They were burning right through his brain...hypnotizing him!

"I'm...I'm blacking...out," Cyclops said as he collapsed.

When he came to, he was lying on the floor—and two police officers were standing over him.

"On your feet, Cyclops," said one. "You're coming with us."

The other officer sighed. "I never thought the day would come when I'd arrest a member of the X-Men for murder."

"*Murder?*" said Cyclops. And then he saw the Pharaoh lying next to him. Dead.

Cyclops scanned the chamber. Alex was gone.

"You're going to have to forgive me, gentlemen," he said as he shot a gentle optic blip at the officers, rendering them unconscious. "When I find my brother, I'll make it up to you."

A few minutes later, Cyclops found a hidden tunnel directly underneath the chamber. "Catacombs," he said to himself. "Alex must have discovered them too."

He started down the tunnel. Suddenly, in the distance, he saw a figure coming towards him. "Alex!" he called.

But it wasn't Alex. It was the Pharaoh!

"You?" said Cyclops. "But you're dead!"

"Exactly what I wish the infidels to believe," answered the Pharaoh. He raised a large ankh, the Egyptian symbol of life, and—*zzzzrok!* An energy blast shot out of it.

Cyclops dodged the powerful ray. But he couldn't use his full force to fight the Pharaoh. He needed him alive.

"What have you done with my brother?" demanded Cyclops, avoiding another blast.

"The same that I will do with you!" said the Pharaoh as he swung his ankh and—*thunkk!*—knocked Cyclops out cold.

When the X-Man opened his eyes, it was pitch-black and the floor beneath him was vibrating. He heard the roar of engines and the distinct sound of an airplane taking off. His head throbbed. "There's some sort of skintight hood," he said aloud, feeling his face, "covering my whole head!"

"A sensible precaution against your mutant powers," said a voice from beside him. "As

you'll see, it is impossible for you to remove it. And please," he said with a laugh, "no cries for help. We are on a private plane. No one can save you now." Cyclops listened as the man walked away.

A heavy door thudded shut. But then Cyclops heard something else. A faint cry for help coming from—he felt around the cargo hold—from a mummy case!

"It's Alex!" said Cyclops. "He's locked inside!"

But with his eyes covered by the hood, there was nothing Cyclops could do but wait.

Several hours later, the plane landed on a private airstrip in Egypt, and Cyclops was led deep inside an ancient tomb. Alex, still in the mummy case, was carried in beside him.

"You and the one called Alex must die," said the Pharaoh, "so that I can assume your powers." The evil mutant aimed his ankh at a statue of a cat, and water began streaming from its mouth. "And now, if you'll excuse me...I must prepare myself for the transfer of power."

The Pharaoh was gone. Cyclops and the mummy case were left alone in the flooding room.

"We're in big trouble," said Cyclops, tugging at the hood. "Unless...Wait a minute!"

Crack! Cyclops splintered the ancient, rotting mummy case with his head.

Alex jumped out of the case. He was all right! The two brothers struggled to remove the hood from Cyclops' head. Finally, after they located a secret zipper, the X-Man was freed.

The brothers made their way out of the pyramid. But there were guards posted outside— dozens of them. Too many for Cyclops and Alex to take on alone.

But then, from out of nowhere, appeared the X-Men! Jean had used her psionic powers to track the brothers down.

"Thank goodness!" Cyclops said to himself. Alex was holding his own, using his fists. But without any mutant power to help him...

"Scott...all of you!" shouted Alex. "Look up there!"

The Pharaoh was poised on a ledge on the side of the pyramid. "Let my deadly ankh be the weapon that destroys both brothers!" he cried, raising the ankh high above his head.

"Stop!!!" cried Alex. And as he waved his arms, a stinging blast of cosmic energy shot from his hands, sending the Pharaoh hurtling to the ground!

"Flee, my warriors," ordered the Pharaoh as he stumbled away, weakened. "My power is gone. Flee, until I summon you once more!" The warriors scattered.

Alex stared at his hands unbelievingly. He held them out to his brother. "Scott? What...what's happening to me?" he asked.

"Don't you see, Alex?" said Cyclops. "Don't you realize?

"In a moment of stress, you revealed an awesome power you never knew you had. That can only mean one thing. It won't be an easy life for you. It isn't for any of us. There are problems... with humans...among ourselves. But you..."

Cyclops paused and took a deep breath.

"*You*—Alex Summers—are a mutant! You absorb your powers from cosmic rays in the universe, as does the Pharaoh, but you have a choice—to use them for good or for evil. The Pharaoh wanted to get rid of you to further his own evil purposes."

The new mutant, who would soon be known to the world as Havok, grasped his brother's hand. "I've made my choice. I choose to be a member of the X-Men." And Havok knew that whatever trials and enemies he might face, he would never have to face them alone.